ShAPeSViLLE

Andy Mills and Becky Osborn
Illustrated by Erica Neitz

gürze books

Gürze Books
P.O. Box 2238
Carlsbad, CA 92018
(760) 434-7533
www.gurze.com

Design by Abacus Graphics, Oceanside, CA

Library of Congress
Cataloging-in-Publication Data

Mills, Andy, 1979-
     Shapesville / Andy Mills and Becky Osborn ; illustrated by Erica Neitz.-- 1st ed.
        p. cm.
     Summary: A celebration of the many different sizes, shapes, and colors of the
people who live in Shapesville, where everyone is different and each is a star.
Includes discussion questions and a note to parents and educators.
     ISBN 0-936077-47-6 (hardcover) -- ISBN 0-936077-44-1 (trade pbk. : alk. paper)
     1. Body image in children--Juvenile literature. [1. Body image.] I.Osborn, Becky.
II. Neitz, Erica, ill. III. Title.
     BF723.B6M55 2003
     306.4'61--dc21
                                              2003012077

9 8 7 6 5 4 3

To my parents, John & Jan,
and my sister, Laura
— Andy —

For my family: Laurie, Wendy,
Erik, Kris, and Erin Osborn
— Becky —

For my bucko cheesehead
— Erica —

Just down the road
not too far away
is a place called Shapesville
where lots of ShAPEs play.

In Shapesville it doesn't matter
what size, shape, or color you are
because here everyone is a star!
Whether you are large, medium, or small,
very short or extremely tall,
come one, come all
and join us friend
we'll have a ball,
and in the end
you might even learn a thing or two
about liking yourself
because you are you!

In Shapesville it doesn't matter
what size, shapE, or color you are . . .
just ask Robbie the Rectangle —
he's an artistic star.

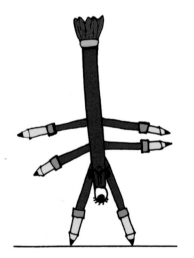

Robbie
is red
and knows
he is tall,
has one eye
on his head
and is great
friends
with all.

In Shapesville it doesn't matter
what size, ShApE, or color you are . . .
just ask Cindy the circle —
she's a movie star.

Cindy
is bright yellow
and uniquely round,
she always says hello
with confidence
abound.

In Shapesville it doesn't matter
what size, SHaPE, or color you are . . .
just ask Tracy the triangle —
she's a basketball star.

Tracy
is dark green
and a little bit shy,
but she likes to be seen
with her head held up high.

In Shapesville it doesn't matter
what size, sHape, or color you are . . .
just ask Sam the blue square —
he's a music star.

He's perfectly tall
and equally wide,
and best of all
Sam's happy inside.

In Shapesville it doesn't matter
what size, SHAPe, or color you are . . .
just ask Daisy the orange diamond —
she's an academic star.

Daisy
loves to read
books and is super
smart, doesn't fret about
her looks, for beauty
is in her
heart.

In Shapesville it doesn't matter
what size or ShApE you are now . . .
just ask our friends —
they will tell you how
happy and healthy
YOUR shape can be.
Just try all the food groups
and you too will see!

Take care of your body,
love it, have fun,
for we all are unique,
whether we bike, swim, or run.
Just do what you like
and like what you do,
go find an exercise
that's just right for YOU!

So tell all your friends,
whatever sHaPe they may be,
that what matters most
may not be on TV.
It's not the size of your ShapE
or the shApE of your size,
but what's in your heart
that deserves first prize.

Be proud of your body
any size, sHapE, or color will do —
be proud of your body
because YOU are a star, too!

Discussion Questions

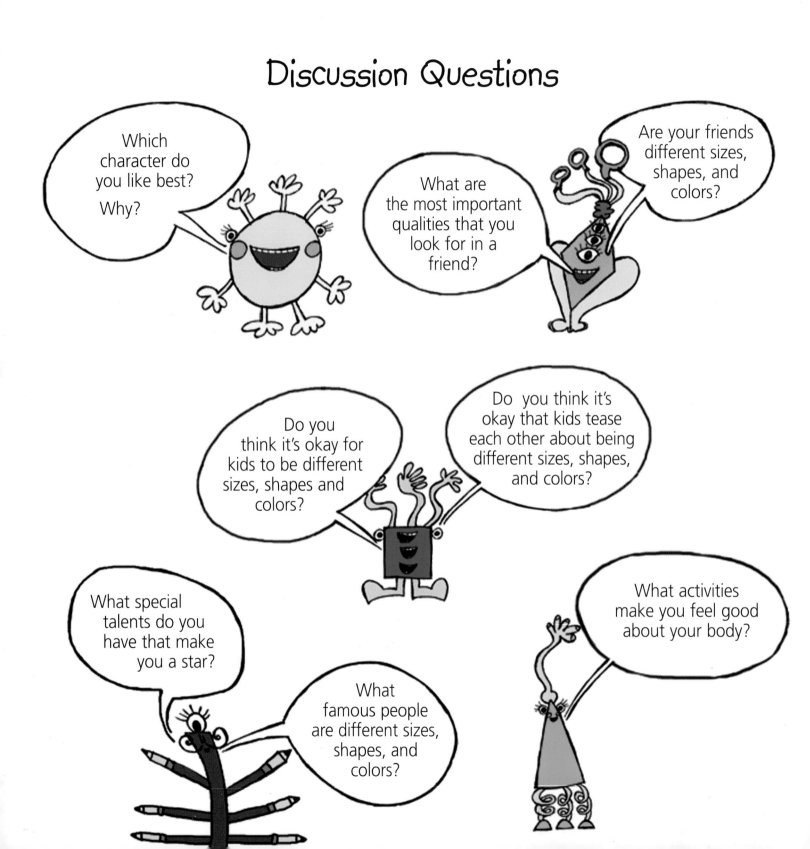

A Note to Educators, Parents, and Others:

At very young ages, today's children become aware that our culture has standards regarding body size, shape, and color. They also develop an awareness of how others, particularly their peers, view them based on these standards. Often, when they don't look like the ideal shown on television or in magazines and other forms of media, kids become embarrassed about their bodies. Teasing of both boys and girls is a common occurrence, with negative consequences for all.

Shapesville is a book about self-acceptance, diversity, and learning to appreciate our differences as individuals. It is meant to be a tool for initiating discussion between adults and children about body image, self-esteem, color differences, and the false belief that an "ideal" body leads to happiness and success. We encourage teachers, parents, and anyone else who influences children to incorporate *Shapesville* into their lesson plans, story times, and even mealtime conversations! Ask your child what he or she thinks of the characters, the story, and what it means to love one's self. Ask yourself whether you are accepting of your own body and how that might impact the children in your care.

The reality is that healthy bodies come in all sizes and shapes. Instilling this idea at an early age will help prevent future body dissatisfaction, unnecessary dieting, eating disorders, and intolerant attitudes and behaviors. Although body love and diversity are not concepts that can be learned by simply reading a picture book, they can be introduced to children as a crucial foundation for self-esteem.

Thank you for making a difference in the world — one child at a time!

Andy, Becky, and Erica

Acknowledgements

Andy, Becky, and Erica would like to thank the following individuals:

Michael Levine, Linda Smolak, Sarah Murnen, Rita Ball, Deb Whitmore,
Keri-Lee Halkett and Fox News Philadelphia, Sue Riggs, David Sarwer,
Lynn Riggenbauch and the staff at Wiggin Street Elementary School,
Cindy Miller and the staff at Elmwood Elementary School,
Barry and Kay Gunderson, the Thomas-Dornhoefer family,
John "Dartman" Wadsworth, Bonnie Pryor,
Dan Laskin and the Kenyon College Alumni Office,
Ruth Woehr and the Kenyon College Counseling Center,
Claudia Esslinger, Jessica Neitz, and most notably,
Francie Droll and John Webster, at Abacus Graphics
and Lindsey Hall and Leigh Cohn, at Gürze Books.

♥

The Story Behind Shapesville

Andy Mills and Becky Osborn met at Kenyon College in Gambier, OH, where they were psychology students studying body image issues in children. Under the guidance of Linda Smolak, Ph.D., an expert on the prevention of eating disorders and body image dissatisfaction, and Sarah Murnen, Ph.D., a specialist in women's issues, Andy and Becky embarked on ten months of intensive research with librarians, teachers, professors, and especially kids. They also investigated children's publishing and discovered few books on this topic.

Andy Mills
Columbus, OH

Andy and Becky then began to write *Shapesville* as an independent study project under the supervision of Michael Levine, Ph.D., an internationally-respected authority on eating disorders prevention. They focused on key areas of diversity: size, shape, and color. After interviewing several illustrators, they selected Erica Neitz, who had graduated from Kenyon the year before and was working at the college. Her bold, whimsical style fit the *Shapesville* story perfectly. With the approval of academic advisors, school counselors and administrators, Andy and Becky continued their research by taking *Shapesville* to classrooms, where it received an overwhelmingly positive response from children, teachers, and staff.

Soon after, Michael Levine showed *Shapesville* to Leigh Cohn, publisher of Gürze Books, a company that has specialized in eating disorders publications and education since 1980. Leigh and his wife, Lindsey Hall, loved it so much that they chose the project as Gürze's first children's book. They worked closely with Andy and Becky, who had recently graduated from Kenyon, Erica, book designers from Abacus Graphics, educators, and numerous prevention specialists to create this much-needed resource for young children.

Becky Osborn
Holyoke, MA

Erica Neitz
Toledo, OH

Additional copies of Shapesville
can be ordered from:

Gürze Books
P.O. Box 2238
Carlsbad, CA 92018
(760) 434-7533
Fax (760) 434-5476
www.gurze.com

$14.95 Hardcover
$7.95 Paperback
Quantity discounts available.